T0354973

PETITE PARLEY

PETITE
PARLEY

WALKER BRYANT

PETITE PARLEY

iUniverse books may be ordered through booksellers or by contacting:

iUniverse
1663 Liberty Drive
Bloomington, IN 47403
www.iuniverse.com
844-349-9409

Because of the dynamic nature of the Internet, any web addresses or links contained in this book may have changed since publication and may no longer be valid. The views expressed in this work are solely those of the author and do not necessarily reflect the views of the publisher, and the publisher hereby disclaims any responsibility for them.

Photograph by author.

ISBN: 978-1-6632-7035-1 (sc)
ISBN: 978-1-6632-7036-8 (e)

Print information available on the last page.

iUniverse rev. date: 02/18/2025

Contents

PART III: SOME PROSE

PART I

Some Forms

CHU CHAI (FREE VERSE)

The human face can be thought of itself as an oil painting, a true work of art. ... A beautiful face will never be denied or ignored.
~ Steven M. Hoefflin, M.D. F.A.C.S.

A Beautiful Face

—————

Once brown your face
Stayed smooth, round, beloved.
The pustules marked the end of childhood.
A red rash flashed like wings on fire
Athwart your cheeks, across your nose.
One day you heard a doctor say:

*I will make it lovely. With precision based
on math and science for the artist and the surgeon,
I will sculpt your face into a work of art in my own image.*

Then I will be loved, you said.

Now converted and camera-ready, your face
Betrayed of math and science and manifest
You hid the scalpel's sin
and wore your burden still.

The *chui chai* poetic form is described as Asian poems of transformation from Thailand. They are performed in Thai classical theater as a transformation song in a solo performance by an actor who portrays "a character who has just changed his or her physical appearance, either cosmetically—into a superlative form of him or herself—or magically, into another figure altogether. The piece comes in two movements, first slow and then fast, and the accompanying lyrics, sung by a chorus offstage, describe the successful metamorphosis," according to Noh Anothai, writing for Sundress Blog (https://sundressblog.com/tag/chui-chai/)

Anothai explains that a chui chai has no meaning other than to announce that "a chui chai [or transformation song] is about to take place."

Source: Paper presented at the 4th Annual Midyear Conference for Fulbright Students and Scholars in Southeast Asia, March 2012, Hanoi Vietnam.

Hurricane Milton

———

Wildly blew the wind
Tangled yellow fronds bow down
The palm lashed and splayed

The Dandelion

———

The dandelion can be dismembered in a child's breath. Once it wore a yellow bonnet. Now, its head is fuzz and frizz, and wispy. And time has stripped it of adornment. Like youth, it was never meant to last.

Crowning hair, thinning
Spring flowering so fleeting
It has sown its seed

You would not have envied a tenor in an overcoat of camel hair had you guessed his fear and known how he would die.
~ Mikhail Bulgakov

The Tenor

——

When she was 92, the teacher spoke
of how well she knew the boy and his joy:
I remember his eyes, he was happy, so happy
to play with his friends; he had a slight stammer,
and an excellent ear, a pitch perfect song
and I am bothered; he had no time to learn relationships.
　　　Social skills, the Fellows mutter.
My heart ached for him . . . he just had to leave all...that behind.
that bothered me; he had no time to learn relationships
how you play . . . that's the way you find out
but he had no time.
　　　Like Citizen Kane, the Fellows utter.
Yearning for *Rosebud*. Bring him to market. Sign here.
Sell him like Joseph, son of Jacob.
Trapped, the mantle wrapped like wire.
　　　Oh my God. What did I do? the Tenor said.
Lay him on the altar.
He is a vegetable.
Eyes pry open his life.
A grand feast served
at the banquet table.
Revelers gorge,
with open throats.
Who will shelter him when the pain
thunders?
　　　And Joseph, who once played guitar,

continued)

echoes:
    Oh, I see you gained a few pounds.
And the boy pledged he would not eat.
    I deal with this anorexia thing, the Tenor said.
I feel sad.
The brothers taunt him. And Joseph too, Oh, you're so
black . . . such a big nose.
So, the Tenor hated the tyrant, who once boxed in the ring,

his stern command, and the sting of the rod in his hand.
The Tenor pledged he would not sing.
Drilled ten years to anxiety.
Purified ten thousand hours.
Polished for pathology.
Grinded to journeyman mastery.
    Perfectionism, the Clinicians proclaim.
Do you know what you did to me? the Tenor cried.
How was a father to know?
No path, no map, no lesson from Leopold
    Like Mozart, the Fellows observe.
Amade, prodigy, fill in the blank, a boy
without peer, R&B will not hold him.
How will he be sheltered, so his gift does not blind us?
Nor his brilliance be bludgeoned. Who will shelter him
when danger enthralls, he, a young fool?
    Like Martini and Haydn to Amade,
Mr. B and Q are to the Tenor and thrill at the joy
of such an astonishing boy, and sharpen him
ten years more as the squire. Draped
and shielded, then knighthood bestowed,
his song a sword, his dance a demand.
    And I have wanted it, I have wanted it, the Tenor enjoined.
    Flow, the Masters exclaim.
The queen in the royal court welcomes him,
the prince and the princess, too.

continued)

The sultans and the sons of sultans,
and kings, and sheiks, and potentates,
heads of state and presidents.
        I'm Peter Pan, I can do anything,
        watch me fly, the Tenor sang.
Each feat as if on a high wire,
Each swagger a strut with no net
The silken sigh of his voice billows,
like sand and storm to warn
of the mirage. A melody plows up
stony hearts.
The mirror reflects
hardened faces,
jutted jaws clinch with envy.
The breaking of the hearts, the Tenor cried.
That's what I don't know how to handle.
Who is it that lacks wisdom?
She alone is *Invincible.* Her understanding
will be your stout steed, her knowledge
the path to your shelter.
        She dares to warn like Bathsheba.
Enchanted ones will besiege you:
Your sweet, spicy scent engulfs them,
with orange flower singing notes
in civet and ambergris.
At the foot of your image, your lovely ones faint.
        Let us hear your voice, cry mothers,
their sons and their daughters, and the father
whose dream is deferred.
Restless fingers glide along counters
as if to draw maps to conduct you.
Hungering eyes seek you at sealed doors,
expecting the knock surely,
when night has fallen.
Dreams deferred will pierce you.
There was no reason you had to stop calling.

continued)

And in the year of his Jubilee,
his image tarnished and torn,
he drank in atonement and liberty, but
the scribes pondered if he was forlorn:
How does it feel to be 50? They inquired:
What will you do on this day?
I feel very wise and sage...very young, the Tenor said.
And, oh, I'll watch some cartoons and eat cake.
But wisdom had touched the Tenor too late.
What price the scepter? What recompense the spectacle?
Such pathos. Yet, what glory.
We, the living, will not see it again.

NOTES ON THE TENOR

The Jacksons, My family, Katherine Jackson, with Richard Wiseman (1990). New York: St Martins Mass Market Paper.

Salvation Army pants

In her memoir, Michael Jackson's mother, Katherine Jackson, wrote that when the family lived in Gary, Indiana, she shopped at Salvation Army to buy secondhand clothing for her nine children (she also sewed).

Joseph the steelworker, the Golden Gloves boxer who played guitar in a band

Joseph worked as a crane operator at Inland Steel in Gary. The working-class family certainly lived modestly but was not impoverished. The hard times came during factory layoffs which happened commonly in fall right before the winter holiday season as production slowed down and having nine children. Joseph also boxed in the Golden Gloves and played guitar in a local R&B band called the Falcons.

Triple bunk

Jermaine Jackson talked about how he and the Jackson brothers shared a triple bunk during their childhood in Gary, Indiana. Their small wooden house on the corner was only about 800 square feet, with two bedrooms and one bath. Sleeping with the kids from an African American viewpoint https://youtu.be/i2g5krXazYs/

Glazed and powdered donuts

Michael's oldest sister, called Rebbie, said their father, Joseph, showed them his love in various little ways, like when he came home from work sometimes with a big sack of donuts for the children.

No lesson from Leopold

Leopold Mozart is known to have rigorously trained his son, Wolfgang Amadeus Mozart, to perform once he realized he was gifted. Amadeus is considered the gold standard for child prodigies. Leopold marketed his son as well.

Like Mozart, the Fellows observe. (The Fellows are a metaphor for scholars)

Georgetown University scholar and author Dr. Michael Eric Dyson, said of Jackson, People have to remember that he was a prodigy at four-to-five years old. Folk would have to think back to the great composer, Mozart, to understand what that means. http://www.finalcall.com/artman/publish/National_News_2/The_life_and_legacy_of_a global_music_icon.shtml

Mozart: A Life, Maynard Solomon (1995). New York, New York: Harper Perennial.

"I remember his eyes"
> Kindergarten teacher recalls MJ school days
> http://abclocal.go.com/story?section=news/someone_you_should_know&id=6903467

> http://ishare.rediff.com/video/entertainment/kindergarten-teacher-recalls-mj-school-days/643734

Social skills
> Laura E. Berk, *Child Development, Eighth Edition*, Eastern Economy Edition, PHI Learning, Allyn & Bacon (2008)

Yearning for *Rosebud*
> In the famous 1941 movie, *Citizen Kane* by Orson Welles, Rosebud was the name of the sled from Kane's childhood in Colorado — a time when he was happy. https://en.wikipedia.org/wiki/Citizen_Kane#.22Rosebud.22

"O my God, what did I do?"
> This is what Jackson told Boteach he said to himself when he realized he was locked into a career (by contract) before he was a teenager. He had missed his childhood and couldn't go back, at least not then. (Boteach, p. 73).
>
> The quotes from these tapes (which were recorded with Jackson's permission) are found in their entirety in *The Michael Jackson tapes: A tragic icon reveals his soul in intimate conversation*. Rabbi S Boteach (2009). New York, NY: Vanguard Press.

"Oh, I see you gained a few pounds"
> Jackson is telling Glenda Stein what Joe Jackson once said to him. Michael Jackson was heard speaking on the phone to Glenda Stein while being secretly recorded by her husband, Sam (now deceased) between 1990-1992: The Stein family uploaded the tapes in 2005 during Jackson's trial http://rhythmofthetide.com/category/glenda-tapes/glenda-transcript-2-2-glenda-tapes/

"This anorexia thing"

Jackson would refuse to eat at times due to psychological distress and had possibly been diagnosed with the disorder. He tells Glenda: "And then I deal with this anorexia thing."

Michael Jackson was heard speaking on the phone to Glenda Stein while being secretly recorded by her husband, Sam (now deceased) between 1990-1992: The conversions have been available on the internet since 2005.
http://rhythmofthetide.com/category/glenda-tapes/glenda-transcript-2-2-glenda-tapes/
Stein Family article with photo of Glenda and Jackson
http://rhythmofthetide.com/glenda-stein-tapes-and-michael-jackson-backstory/

Castro, J., Araceli, G., Gual, P., Lahortiga, F., Saura, B., Toro, J. (2003). Perfectionism dimensions in children and adolescents with anorexia nervosa. *Journal of Adolescent Health,* 2004; 35:392-398

"Oh, you're so black/your nose is so big"

Jackson is telling Glenda Stein this is what Joe Jackson would say to him. The phrase about so *black* has been cut out on the transcript, but was heard on the recording.
http://rhythmofthetide.com/category/glenda-tapes/glenda-transcript-2-2-glenda-tapes/

Drilled ten years to anxiety

The rigid training Joe imposed as an authoritarian parent *may* have led to perfectionism and possibly anxiety disorder in Michael, as well as anorexia. According to Harvard psychologist, Howard Gardner, prodigies emerge before the age of ten and develop in ten year increments, with the first breakthrough that takes the world by storm, so to speak, in their early twenties.

Howard Gardner, H. (1998). *Extraordinary minds: portraits of extraordinary individuals and an examination of our extraordinariness.* London: Phoenix.

Perfectionism, the Clinicians exclaim. (The Clinicians are a metaphor for psychologists)

Castro, J., Araceli, G., Gual, P., Lahortiga, F., Saura, B., Toro, J. (2003). Perfectionism dimensions in children and adolescents with anorexia nervosa. *Journal of Adolescent Health,* 2004; 35:392-398.

"Do you know what you did to me?"
    This is what Jackson told Boteach he wanted to tell Joseph about what he had suffered from his father as a child. The quotes from these tapes (which were recorded with Jackson's permission) are found in their entirety in *The Michael Jackson tapes: A tragic icon reveals his soul in intimate conversation.* Rabbi S Boteach (2009). New York, NY: Vanguard Press.
http://www.wired.com/2011/12/neurology-of-abuse/

Like Martini and Haydn
Mozart: A Life, Maynard Solomon (1995). New York, New York: Harper Perennial.

Mr. B and Q
    Michael's nicknames for Berry Gordy and Quincy Jones

Ten years the squire
Second ten year period before first breakthrough for creative artists.

Howard Gardner, H. (1998). *Extraordinary minds: portraits of extraordinary individuals and an examination of our extraordinariness.* London: Phoenix.

David Nordahl, Artist (painted Jackson being knighted).
http://www.fanpop.com/clubs/michaeljackson/images/15740943/title/david-nordahl-fanart

http://www.michaeljacksonart.com/domains/
michaeljacksonart.com/details.php?image_id=20

http://www.telegraph.co.uk/news/picturegalleries/
celebritynews/6780114/Michael-Jackson-art-paintings-
by-David-Nordahl-and-portraits-and-sculptures-by-other-
artists.html?image=9

"And I have wanted it, I have wanted it"
Jackson tells Boteach that he wanted the fame and success because he wanted to be loved. The quotes from these tapes (which were recorded with Jackson's permission) are found in their entirety in *The Michael Jackson tapes: A tragic icon reveals his soul in intimate conversation.* Rabbi Schumley Boteach (2009). New York, NY: Vanguard Press.

Flow, the Masters exclaim. (The Masters are a metaphor for creative artists)
Creativity: Flow and the Psychology of Discovery and Invention,
Mihaly Csikszentmihalyi (1996). New York: Harper Perennial.

"I'm Peter Pan"
Jackson is seen in this YouTube video singing the theme song to *Peter Pan*, the movie. He is about 24 years old and lives at home with Joe and Katherine. This is from an unauthorized interview in 1983 at the Jackson family home. Here is what he is singing "Dancing on a cloud...soaring up so high. Watch me now...watch me fly! I'm Peter Pan! I can do anything. I soar so high! I am forever!" https://youtu.be/ThKabNWorn4

As if on a high wire/no net
This is what real estate broker Gloria Rhoads Berlin wrote that Jackson told her when she was working with him to find and purchase the Neverland Valley Ranch property.

Michael Jackson: In Search of Neverland, Gloria Rhoads Berlin, (2010). Gloria Rhoads Publications.

"The breaking of the hearts"

"I don't like to break hearts. I don't really know these people and, gosh, it's a weird thing. That, I think, is the weird part about show business. You portray an image. And those people are into you so long, buying your records. You're all over their walls. They wake up seeing you. They go to sleep seeing you. They wake up thinking about you. You're totally on their mind. And when they meet you in person, they feel they have been knowing you for a long time. But I don't know them. You see, that's the painful part of show business –the breaking of the hearts. Do you know what that does to them? God, some of them go to the point of committing suicide because they get real serious. That's what I don't know how to handle." - **Michael Jackson,** *Jet* **1979 (Talking of obsessive fans)** *By Robert E. Johnson / JET Associate Publisher* https://floacist.wordpress.com/2007/10/20/jet-interview-august-16-1979/

"How does it feel to be 50?"
"I feel very wise and sage," Jackson said.
http://abcnews.go.com/GMA/SummerConcert/story?id=5680705&page=1

—◠◠—

Folkway Singalong

I got my transistor with me on the bus
All the while, I sing along
I got my books with me in my room
All the while, I read alone

All the while, I sing along
Change is on the way Cook sings
All the while, I read alone
Crispus Attucks, it was segregated

Change is on the way Cook sings
Black Gloria bussed to integrate
Crispus Attucks, it was segregated
White Glenda bussed to integrate

Black Gloria bussed to integrate
Liberation learning left behind
White Glenda bussed to integrate
Social justice steered the course

Liberation learning left behind
And if Pete Seeger had a hammer
Social justice steered the course
For unions and a living wage

And if Pete Seeger had a hammer
Solidarity is key
For unions and a living wage
Dear ecology, Marvin crooned for mercy

(continued)

Solidarity is key
Diana birthed Berry's love child
Dear ecology, Marvin crooned for mercy
Motown was Diana's social justice

Diana birthed Berry's love child
No need to cry for them
Motown was Diana's social justice
The Monkees droned dark clouds descending

No need to cry for them
Long-haired Cowsills mock hypocrisy
The Monkees droned dark clouds descending
And all the while I sang along

Long-haired Cowsills mock hypocrisy
Proud James heralded blackness loud
All the while I sang along
Janis was but seventeen and sad

Proud James heralded blackness loud
Aretha chanted for respect
Janis was but seventeen and sad
Society forbade Black love sang Janis

Aretha chanted for respect
Goodbye, Mama, you had surely known
Society forbade Black love sang Janis
White mothers sometimes die alone

Goodbye, Mama, you had surely known
Confusion reigned as one big ball when I was seventeen
White mothers sometimes die alone
Sons with guns and soldiers gone to war

(continued)

Confusion reigned as one big ball when I was seventeen
Along came Sly and The Family Stone
Sons with guns and soldiers gone to war
Everyday people will march no more

Along came Sly and The Family Stone
Arlo, Woody's son, called out the hypocrisy
Everyday people will march no more
And fools will strain at gnats

Arlo, Woody's son, called out hypocrisy
Marvin wants to holler o'er the inner city
And fools will strain at gnats
Fifth Dimension sings to save the country

Marvin wants to holler o'er the inner city
The Osmonds heavy metal air pollution
Fifth Dimension sings to save the country
I had my radio and I sang along

The Osmonds heavy metal air pollution
Mr. Mayfield caroled strength and hope
I had my radio and I sang along
Suburbs, here we come

Mr. Mayfield caroled strength and hope
He was a do right man who died while young
Suburbs, here we come
The joy now gone, Grace sang we all need love

He was a do right man who died while young
Carly serenaded we must marry, no?
The joy now gone, Grace sang we all need love
Mama wore her boots when she walked out

(continued)

Carly serenaded we must marry, no?
Sundays spent in Pleasantville
Mama wore her boots when she walked out
Driving to the city on a concrete ring,

Sundays spent in Pleasantville
Children learned in pleasant schools
Driving to the city on a concrete ring,
Past the inner city blues

Children learned in pleasant schools
When the yellow torrent flooded
Past the inner city blues
Black children bussed to pleasant schools

When the yellow torrent flooded
Balls of confusion the Temptations rapped
Black children bussed to pleasant schools
Black parents moved to subdivisions

Balls of confusion the Temptations rapped
White parents dug up the fields and built new homes
Black parents moved to subdivisions
Everyone has credit

White parents dug up the fields and built new homes
Now everyone has debt
Everyone has credit
Now they own you, Leslie Gore

Now everyone has debt
Throw up two hands and holler
Now they own you, Leslie Gore
And we can't pay the taxes

(continued)

And we can't pay the taxes
Now we're stuck on sodded ranches
Throw up two hands and holler
Our paychecks never match up

Our paychecks never match up
The credit keeps on coming
Now we're stuck on sodded ranches
We shop the big box market

The credit keeps on coming
We are conspicuous consumers
We shop the big box market
Good capitalists are we

We are conspicuous consumers
Don't need no critical thought
Good capitalists are we
We need our guns in stores and schools

Don't need no critical thought
Conscientization is unamerican
Just need our guns in stores and schools
Liberation is too Freirean

Conscientization is unamerican
We need workers don't ya know
Liberation is too Freirean
And worker wages low

We need workers don't ya know
Highlander is burning
And worker wages low
Just not those union folk

(continued)

Highlander is burning
Training leaders don't ya see
Just not those union folk
The truth will set them free

Training leaders don't ya see
It's almost biblical to me
The truth will set them free
What do we do you ask?

It's almost biblical to me
Disorientation, a dilemma
What do we do, you ask?
Alas, we must change

Disorientation, a dilemma
As to Simon Peter the Judean
Alas, we must change
Have no respect of persons

As to Simon Peter the Judean
Peter went to see Cornelius
Have no respect a persons
All justice must be blind

Peter went to see Cornelius
Oppressors are not welcome
All justice must be blind
Let the oppressed go free

Oppressors are not welcome
Peace is a practice
Let the oppressed go free
Knowledge is the key

(continued)

Peace is a practice
Let the teacher then be whole
Knowledge is the key
Let the learner then be whole

Let the teacher then be whole
Thus, get wisdom
Let the learner then be whole
Get understanding too

Thus, get wisdom
She is the wellspring of implicitness
Get understanding too
The fountain of free thinking

She is the wellspring of implicitness
Blind truth is buried in her folds
The fountain of free thinking
Justice is the banner

Blind truth is buried in her folds
We demand that we be told the truth
Justice is the banner
We must teach it far and wide

We demand that we be told the truth
We were young then
We must teach it far and wide
We are our parents now

We were young once
I had my books with me in my room
We are our parents now
I had my transistor with me on the bus

Children Not White

———

In search of surviving white mothers
whose journey has landed uncertain
who were gentle
with children not white
but with children whose hair
would always be bushy

Hair that would always be bushy
to frustrate gentle white mothers
but with children whose hair
and whose lives had arrived uncertain
these children not white
who were also like her and gentle

For the thing which I greatly feared is come upon me,
and that which I was afraid of is come unto me
~ Job 3.25 (KJV)

Pride Before the Fall

———

Before the fall, I fumed; I turned aside.
Good Job confessed he fell because of fear.
For me, it was my arrogance and pride.

Before the fall, when counsel was supplied,
I veered away and would not give an ear.
Before the fall, I fumed; I turned aside.

"O, dear daughter," my father came beside.
"I have provided; now my wisdom hear."
For me, it was my arrogance and pride.

O, my dear wife," my woeful husband sighed.
"I will leave you. Do let this truth be clear."
Before the fall, I fumed; I turned aside.

Before the fall, these dry eyes had not cried.
I will not care at all should he leave here.
For me, it was my arrogance and pride.

Now my love is gone; He does not reside.
I have no child. That truth is in each tear.
Before the fall, I fumed; I turned aside.
For me, it was my arrogance and pride.

Reflection on the Villanelle Form

——

It is true that you cannot *narrate* your story in villanelle form. It seems, the form will only let you repeat an evocative statement and the story reveals itself in the form. The central theme of this villanelle is hubris, its consequences, and the resulting loss it can cause. In the poem, I reveal at the beginning that I am the narrator and the subject. And, I add losses so they add up like they did with Job (though his losses were incomparably massive and tragic). Whether I could have written this poem without the villanelle form is hard to determine. I'm inclined to think not. We know unspeakable truth comes out often in poetry, whether one likes it or not. Perhaps the form refused to let me cover myself in metaphor, but required I look in the mirror at my own culpability in my undoing, as was Job's in his self-fulfilling prophecy about his fear.

Guardian Angels Come and Gone: Situations of Felt Sorrow

———

For over ten years, my brother told everyone that someone was following him. He couldn't understand why and thought that perhaps he had inadvertently picked up some classified information when he was a Marine, though he was only a lance corporal and drove trucks. But maybe they thought he knew something. Or maybe it was his ex-wife. Maybe she was trying to find money to feed the four children she had birthed when they were married, all four children that he fathered. He would stare off as if he saw or heard something. In photographs of him, you can see him doing that, as if in deep thought, even though he held his infant son in his arms or sat among us laughing just moments before. Sometimes he would ask the person sitting next to him if they could hear the voices, too, saying, "Hear it? They're saying I'm a no good bastard, son of bitching faggot," he'd say. And whoever sat next to him would tilt their head and strain trying to hear. The lone eyebrow raised and their ear poised, "No, I don't hear anything, J. D. There's no one there. No one is there," they said.

Then, later we all finally understood, after he had shot himself in the head with a pearl handled 32-caliber pistol notorious for spewing bullets that ricochet through gray matter inside the skull and never exit. And, we were left with all our failures to realize, to understand, to intervene, and to seek help for him. We didn't know. His wife didn't know to keep him on the line and the mobile phone bill with 200 calls to their home in the mountains, each a second and a half apart, just long enough to redial, 200 calls reached a busy signal and its promise that eventually someone would answer, but at about dawn, the night was spent and there was nowhere to go for my brother.

Several years ago, I was touched by the image of the small, dead Syrian child, three years old, whom had washed ashore in Turkey. The child was alone in his death, face down in a puddle of water from the ocean on a resort beachfront. There were more dead scattered about, his mother, his brother. In the photographer's image, the day appeared bright and sunny, with a warm breeze ruffling the hair of the other dead lying face down in the sand, as if resting, or sunbathing, although most of them remained fully clothed. A Turkish rescue worker peered down at the child as he prepared to lift the stiff body. The man was dressed in green-grayish cargo pants blousing over black, latched boots. He wore a red, white, and blue vest, over a pale gray short-sleeve shirt with a yellow emblem on the sleeve. On his head is a green beret. It is a news image, not a painting, not a poem, and I feel sorrow when I think of it. The child is dressed in navy blue cotton shorts and a red cotton shirt. Someone who loved him, almost certainly his mother, had dressed him that morning for the journey to a safe place where they would find refuge. There were 12 of them, in a dinghy, fleeing from Akyarlar trying to cross the Aegean straight to reach the Greek island of Kos. It was only three miles. His name was Aylan Al-Kurdi. Artists have since rendered his image. He had a brother named Ghalib, who was five and who also drowned off the coast of Turkey.

And then there is little eight-year-old Gizzell, the little black girl who was tortured and murdered by her grandmother and father. She wrote of her aspirations: "I am going to be great all day." She wanted to play and go on a field trip with other children. She wanted to sit down and not have to stand in a corner for hours holding a book over her head, with a gag in her mouth to suppress her sobs. She didn't want to "mess up" and be punished more by the grandmother who wore a leather belt around her neck. People who loved her had praised her, calling her "'smart and courageous and beautiful.'" She wrote that she could do anything she put her "'smart mind to.'" But, then she wrote: "Not true . . . I failed."

Situations such as these have caused me sorrow and I am perplexed. It is not as if God mystifies me. I know He sends guardian angels (messengers) and that there is an angel (messenger) of death, not sent by God. So, I am left to wonder where was Alyan's guardian angel? Not so much for my brother because I know that he had received the salvation of God when he was 13 and he made a free will choice to take his life. But, the Alyans of the world hardly had a chance and I am tempted to blame. But, I do not blame God. No. I just wonder. Where was Alyan's and Gizzell's guardian angel? Aren't they always involved when it comes to ministering to those who will be heirs of salvation, according to Hebrews 1:14? Aren't they there to watch over us, to keep us alive, as a ministering spirit until we are able to accept the salvation of God? Alyan and Gizzell hardly had a chance. It's as if an angel had come and gone, and evil crept in unawares and prevailed.

Certainly, we can learn from the ministry of angels. We're on the same team and so they are sent to help, to minister, to deliver messages, and in situations of peril and need they bring God's wisdom, protection, and comfort. They're in the right place at the right time. Their ministries are broad and powerful, and they speak for and represent God in all perfection and power. So where were they for Alyan and Gizzell? How do we make sense of it, without attributing blame where it does not belong?

Angels are spiritual beings that God sends as special representatives to do specific jobs that only they can do. They don't just appear at will; they follow a standard protocol. The word "protocol" is defined in the *Random House Dictionary of the English Language* as "the customs and regulations dealing with diplomatic formality, precedents, and etiquette." So, angels must work within certain boundaries; they have limitations of what is their responsibility just as we do. They validate, sanction, and endorse events that are important for them to carry out on behalf of God. We see this protocol in the social and political realm, such as weddings and inaugurations where, for instance, the bridegrooms and bridesmaids carry out their specific function to support the bride and the groom, and without this support the wedding party would suffer. Likewise, when it comes to the very important event of a presidential inauguration that requires the presence of Members of Congress to witness, the Chief Justice of the Supreme Court to do the swearing-in, and the outgoing president and his wife, and the incoming president and his wife and family. In each case, these important events require the presence of a teammate to perform the functions. For instance, brides need the assistance of the bridesmaids to help prepare for the wedding. It is the same with the heavenly protocol of angels: their presence marks the importance of an occasion and they perform functions that could not otherwise be carried out appropriately to suit the situation. That's why the angels were sent to call Moses to lead the children of Israel out of Egypt and slavery. When Moses saw the burning bush, he turned aside to find out what it was all about. Once he gave attention to this matter, he was able to receive his calling from God to fulfill his mission. The children of Israel were led out of Egypt toward the new land that promised to be appropriate for them to settle in and live well. The angel had been sent to move Moses forward in this mighty mission that would change the course of history. There are many other examples of angel protocol recorded in the Bible.

So, if angels are powerful spiritual beings sent to represent God in important matters; yet, they must follow certain protocols, might we find out a little bit more about their specific duties and their limitations. First, they are sometimes involved in delivering a message of rebuke and corrective instruction as they did when, as recorded in Genesis 22:11 and 12, the angel stopped Abraham from mistakenly sacrificing his son, Isaac. Abraham was willing to do this because he thought it was what God wanted; however, an angel had to come and stop him from making this huge error. In another instance, angels were sent as messengers to instruct Gideon, a man of valor, to rescue Israel from an enemy camp. Finally, sometimes angels are commissioned to administer consequences for those resisting God's directives and harming His people. The term "wrath" is used for the built-in effects of violating universal principles, such as violating the principle of gravity by diving head first off the Empire State building. The wrath is the terrible result. Such outcomes, as painful and destructive as they may be, are a part of life. We have all experienced unpleasant consequences for our errors at times. Of course, not all our missteps require the presence of an angel to set us straight, but in some instances, this was exactly what was needed. For instance, in one instance Archangel Michael appeared with his sword drawn and announced that he was the captain of the host of the Lord who had come to lead Joshua to the military victory that captured Jericho. Indeed, the scope and power and range of the ministry of these angels and the boundaries of their influence is hard to comprehend, but, again, they do have boundaries and there are things they can't do. Those are things that we have been given the responsibility to carry out.

Finally, there is one area that involves salvation in which "guardian angels" are always involved, according to Hebrews 1:14. They are "ministering spirits" that are sent out to "minister" for the people God knows will believe and be saved, so that the enemy of God's people can't destroy them before they have a chance to hear and believe. According to Scripture, not all people on earth are in that category, however. So, what does that mean for Alyan and Gizzell, two little children who hardly had a chance? I'm convinced there will come a day when I'll find the answer to this question. I'm sure there are some sensible answers, but there are things that at present we haven't learned or just can't know. It will just have to be enough for now to know that angels are in the right place at the right time, and according to protocol, for the right reason.

Mackey, Robert (2015, Sept. 2). "Brutal Images of Syrian Boy Drowned Off Turkey Must Be Seen, Activists Say." New York Times. https://www.nytimes.com/2015/09/03/

world/middleeast/brutal-images-of-syrian-boy-
drowned-off-turkey-must-be-seen-activists-say.html/

Schmadeke, Steve (2017, Mar. 2). "I hate this life' – Slain girl's
journals focus of grandmother's murder trial." Chicago
Tribune. http://www.chicagotribune.com/news/local/
breaking/ct-grandmother-murder-trial-met-20170302-
story.html/

The Way International. "What God's Word Says About Angels,"
New Knoxville: American Christian Press, 2005.

PART II

Some Poems

Mr. Detroit Walks the Mezzanine

Hart Plaza Downtown Detroit

He came walking slow with a cane held in his white gloved
left hand as if he was the same as he had once been, a white
tie loose a centimeter, a white boutonniere in his right hand,
a canary yellow jacket rests at right angle, a cigarette holder
perched at the corner of his mouth, tension sealed. Teeth startle
the unlit smoke, flip it up like a finger snap, jaw clenched in
a grind as he walks with a dip along the mezzanine. Twitters
in the arena. Collective homage on YouTube:

> playa, playa a cold brotha ice cold real mf playa oooh,
> sugar daddy woman sighs; another: pimp daddy! cat
> daddy grandpa fresh pop cool as hell real swag smooth
> criminal smooth operator smooth fellow mellow yellow
> looks fly majestic as fuck pimpin' ain't easy pimp juice
> dude cool as a mug real deal Bulldog Joe when your
> pimp game is tight swag on a million

He saunters along the steely concrete, past iron banisters and
staggered seats. Honey vanilla hat on 45° tilt, his gossamer
yellow shirt flutters as if caught by a wisp of summer wind;
wide legged pants, fluid and cuffed, draped over black and
white spats. Dapper. Fluted giggles from the bleachers. Folks
in shorts and cotton tops lean forward, arms slung over
railings. Had he come to show how it was before? Had he come
to take one more walk in full regalia? 60 years of knotted tie.
In 1942, after the war, in Washington, D. C., my father stands
on the lawn of Howard University facing the camera wearing

a wine-red zoot suit and pork pie hat. The knotted tie. Then. The era of dapper. The long, manicured nails and curly, black hair of my philandering uncle. The age of the dandy. Muted laughter sails in the air. Rafters hum. Two minutes in camera range Mr. Detroit walks the mezzanine as if his cane was onyx, not wood, as if his gloves were kidskin, not cotton, and his Stacy Adams were fresh, not frayed.

Poppy

Red-poppy bleeds into the jamb, over the joints, into the casing. Red-poppy drips from the head, sprouts from the urn like a shot of Botox, just a bit for immunity. Ward off the angel of death seeping under the sill. Behind the bleeding entrance, a white wall rises on a white windowsill. A narrow window fades to black. Green bushes toil under the darkness. The house next door is surrounded by a fortress of flowering bush to rebel. Reconnoiter seeds creep over to breed in twilight and rise up to choke red poppy. But, no, poppy has been vaccinated and domesticated, no more to be defied than seed on a baker's dozen.

Ah, beloved opioid. American opioid: stay away. You are a conspiracy from abroad to extinguish the Americas, especially America, because America does not want to know. O, Poppy, my Poppy. You have robbed us of your joy, your seducing beauty makes war for opium.

You are a conspiracy of farming to feed families who slave in the field to harvest you. You are a conspiracy to feed oligarchs and kill us all. What does it matter when all the world can be bought, every island, islet, inlet, and every continent? Rape one and then another. For progeny, the mountains bow down. Open and flowering, they await your ascension.

Red splashes the brown, wooden door, red as lamb's blood. The knobbed golden ring will not answer.

Hominy

It was on the shelves at the Tucson grocers where it belongs. Not on the breakfast plate of a runaway of fourteen in Hoosierville juvie. Eat it or mop the floor again. Bland and slimy hominy, corn carbs soaked in limewater. Baby chick yellow. Not yellow like the sunny-side eggs my mother squashed into the plate with her fork. I ate smashed eggs into womanhood, and sopped the mass with buttered salty toast into suburbia. I think of Valisa's glistened calves, her bare legs the summer night she was picked up after curfew when she was seventeen and strolled into the day room as we slapped Spades on the table, her pleated, toffee circle skirt, tight at the waist, sheltering her thighs and her high heels like a woman and how she captivated us with buoyant tales about her pimp Ducky, as if he was her hero. And, at the Tucson grocery, I think of my perplexed, fallen-faced father on visiting day with nickel and dime coin rolls for candy bars, chips, and pop. And I think of Valisa and Ducky, and the patrons of bare-legged, teenage girls in honeyed heels like a woman.

Oligarchy 2025

Kingmakers for the apprentice monarch rush in for reward.
Foolish as a fledgling, he auctions power.
Step up. Oh pray. Mercy spared him.
Why? one wonders, no mercy for the young miss
aflame with zeal.
I'll be there with you, he pledged.
She breathed out among fellows, but not him.
Mercy for the widow and orphans
Covered by the father's lifeblood.
None for him? Why not? one wonders.

We see our descent, we see
They plunder the treasuries
They rocket in space
They pace flush playing fields
Now prove O God of Heaven, You champion
of judgement and justice
Buoy up with joy the disheartened.
Relieve the burdened.
Engorged with greed, let corrupt flesh swallow itself whole.

Don't Come Here Like This

They find them dead in the desert
like the one collapsed against
an Ironwood tree
legs folded sideways
feet stacked in shoes
made for walking, running
Faceless, his back to the camera
a water pouch slung crossways
over adolescent shoulders.
A dry death in the Sonoran Desert.
Are they waiting for word on the other
side?
How long before they know
no word will come, please stop
wade the Rio Grande and live
don't come here like this
to be found in the desert
All hope gone

In the News

Border Patrol officials in the past three months have described multiple rescues along the Arizona border. The most recent example, disclosed Thursday, described two rescues earlier in the week. In the first one from Monday, agents on patrol at the Tohono O'odham Nation encountered and treated an unconscious 20-year-old migrant from Guatemala for severe dehydration.

The next day, agents found two migrants wandering in the desert near Tombstone, in Cochise County. The man was fine, but the 26-year-old woman traveling with him was drifting in and out of consciousness, the Border Patrol said. In both instances, medical crews transported the two unconscious migrants to a nearby hospital via helicopter, often times the easiest and fastest method of transportation, especially in remote areas of the border.

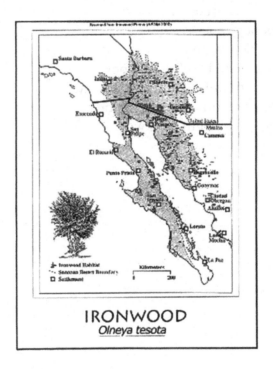

Distribution map of Ironwood Trees

Map courtesy Bill Singleton
Pima County (AZ) Administrative Office

California Fire

Redwood trees winch up spindle limbs
Sending mercy prayers to Nimbus
Woody roots beg relief
Along the creekside door
Saffron sun shines black with soot
ablaze and windswept, thus trees sway.
Overhead, lean clouds drift in silence,
And so some days begin this way.

When the Time Comes

My father, I was sure, would never die. He just kept going, not spritely, of course; in fact he was rickety, all five foot one inch, 104 pounds of him. He coulda, shoulda been a racehorse jockey. He would look like the brown jockey statues that once perched on the manicured lawns where white people lived.

That was before new generations of dark children took issue with brown jockey statues as lawn decorations, though I think of them as a piece of Americana, like the Borden's cow by the railroad tracks in Milwaukee, or a wheel barrel, or a covered bridge. I suppose the children preferred some other ceramic figure like, P.T. Barnum, except he was still alive, or Louie Armstrong, though I don't think he was ready for statuary status either. Still, they were fine riders, those brown, colored, negro—or whatever black was called then—jockeys who won horse races. Fine riders.

And Dad was a soldier once and a psyche major about to graduate from Howard University on the G.I. Bill, though he never did that either. Yet, Sartre's seminal work, *On Being and Nothingness* remained on the bookshelf throughout my childhood. Not like the encyclopedias that were repossessed before Dad could buy them like he said he would. But, when he saw me one day, at about thirteen or so, take down the book to read, he laughed. I never read it. I will miss him when the time comes.

To Die Alone

He waited for me
I told him I would be there
Did I say soon? My defense.
In the morning, a nurse lifted his eighty-eight pound
Skeleton, tube trailing, and propped him in a chair
He bent forward waiting for me
You told me you would be here, he said
My mouth flaps open in useless excuse
He pulls out the hollow tube snaking down his throat
Into his stomach
I'm tired now, he said. A nurse put him back in bed
I plugged his ears with Lionel Ritchie singing
Eyes closed; his body stirred for his last dance
I covered his right hand with my right hand
until he pulled away
I stayed the day until dusk
When his wife came, I left
A nurse stayed the night until dawn

Zippy, Leased New, Then Bought

She drives me flying
Not as fleet as when we first rolled out,
Fast enough
After all, I'm older now.
We wander east,
New York City to Nashville,
back to New York, then Atlanta
back to Tennessee.
We are not in any way having fun
She presses me firm and fast
Abandonment
All these pressing issues

Time's arrow, so difficult to bend...
~ Michael Jackson, Dancing the Dream

The Green of Ireland

He would be alive they say
Had he stayed
On castle grounds
Where kings belong
He would be alive they say
Amidst the green of Ireland

PART III
Some Prose

On Dolls

The doll lies in a cradle in the dim, quiet room. She is clothed in a white, cotton gown. Her hands are pale. Her fleshy feet are bare. I pick her up and cuddle her, squeezing her into my chest, rubbing my cheek against her soft, round face. Her body molds into mine and I imagine this is what a real baby will be like one day. I am surprised at how pleasant it feels. Her face is not plastic like my baby doll at home. I am a little girl. The doll is soft and I can *still feel* how my female child empty womb longed for her to be mine. I carry her into the other room, where my mother and grandmother are talking. I am hesitant, but hopeful.

"Can I have this doll?" I ask my grandmother, Daisy Mae, whom I have only this once ever met or seen on this one and only ever visit to her home. I have a grandfather here, too. But he is not my mother's father. This grandfather adopted my mother and her three sisters, after their father, Lester, committed suicide, and grandmother remarried. They live in a lower-level, two-bedroom apartment underneath the funeral home for which they are the caretakers. Later, I will visit a darkened funeral parlor, where this grandfather, Harold, will lie dead. That is the last I saw of either of them. Before she died, my mother, who didn't live very long, told me Daisy Mae moved to Clinton, Georgia, and died there.

"No," my grandmother says. "The other children might want to play with it, too." The other children are my cousins. I take the baby doll back into the room and lay her on her back in the cradle. I feel an ache inside, a deep pull of yearning, unexplainable to me then, unexplainable to me still. I was nine.

My grandmother and mother sit me on a settee to take a photograph. They give me a porcelain doll dressed in a ruffled, blue ballgown and a stuffed skunk, black with a white stripe and a fluffy tail. The settee is next to a console television set. On the top of the console is a photograph of the other children, my cousins whose names I did not know then and do not know now. It is a photograph of a blonde boy and blonde girl, brother and sister I'm told, who face one another in an endearing pose staged at the professional portrait studio. My mother tells me to smile. In the photograph, I am smiling, one might call it cheerily, my dark, curly hair falls in ringlets around my face. The picture is for my mother's sisters, so they can see, so she can say, "see." She has a little girl with white skin (even though my father was a Black man), just like the sisters do, just like their children. At home, I pick up my baby doll and hold it close to me to cuddle it. It is stiff. The clothing is thin cotton, exposing bare, plastic feet, thighs, buttocks, the belly, the rigid arms; all of it is pale plastic and hard. I toss it in a corner and turn to Nancy Drew and The Hardy Boys. Then my mother gave me a Barbie when I was eleven.

Barbie was blonde like my cousins. Her smooth, cone-shaped breasts stood firm, always. Her waist always cinched, even without a corset pulling it in, like Scarlett O'Hara in *Gone with the Wind,* so that her breasts puffed up like muffins from under her V-neck top. She had muffin-top breasts and slender, hairless legs, her buttocks slightly creased. Her hymen appeared to be outside her labia and stretched from one side of her crotch to the other so that her vagina was hidden. She was not ready for Ken, yet. But when Ken came along, everything changed.

Yes, because Ken and Barbie wrestled around, legs and arms all twisted together. Ken pinned Barbie down as if trying to find a point of penetration before realizing that it wouldn't matter if he did. So, then sometimes he smashed his face and chest into her body, with my fist clamped around his legs, his arms flapping at his sides, and hers flopping on impact. Maybe he was frustrated at his impotence against her resistance. I do not think Barbie was ever a baby doll or even a young child, like me and my cousins. She has no organs for reproduction, so she will always be childless. I will always be childless, too, though I never planned to be, and did not have to be. Somehow, it seems as if I knew even then. It seems I was never ready.

On Bearing Up

My father calls to let me know what happened to Jeffrey. The police have taken him to the hospital after finding him unconscious in his car with a gunshot wound to his head. The surgeon operated on him the nurse tells me when she shows me to his room. My father and his wife are here. Jeff's wife soon arrives from Maryland. Bandages are wrapped around Jeff's head. They look like a 10-gallon turban. He is 5' 10" lying there on his back. He would be 7' if he stood.

"His brain swelled," the doctor says. Jeff is not hooked up to breathing apparatus or life preservation medical devices. The organ donor representative wants to talk to Jeff's wife right away. He is dead but the hospital staff is accommodating the family before the doctor lifts a half-mast eyelid and directs a 2-second light beam at the pupil. The doctor snaps the light off. "No, I'm sorry," he says, without raising his head, and hurries from the room. I feel numb. Yet, like always, I feel resolved to bear up.

I am the oldest sibling in the family and once again I am left to pick up the pieces, like the time when I was 17 and my father sold insurance and went to prison for fraud. He had loaned premium deposits to his brother, Uncle Don, for a short-term investment that didn't pay off. My father took the fall. At the time, their mother, my grandmother, lived with us. And all of us were evicted when the bank foreclosed on the house. The lawyer representing my father came and carried the television and stereo console out of the house in exchange for legal fees. We were all underage, so we needed to find a place to live before social services found out and came for us. Uncle Don said Jeff could come with him, but no; that would be ludicrous. Look what you've done to your own 77 year old mother, who must go live in subsidized housing for the elderly. A friend of my father's took Jeff. I found an apartment to sublet for my other brother and our younger sister. I said I was 19 and began to provide childcare for the army families from nearby Fort Benjamin Harrison that the Clinton administration would close years later. You bear up.

The next day, I arrive at the police pound around noon to collect my brother's personal effects from his vehicle. The police said they put everything back like it was before their investigation, except the cell phone and the gun. They found the car backed up to the cemetery gate, as if it was just a warning and there was still a chance. I pick up the keys at the front desk. "I'll show you where it is," the attendant says. I follow him out into the parking lot, misshapen and unkempt, pierced with grassy ruts and pools of gravel, irregular. He laughs. "Some nut blew his brains out," he says. I blink. He must think I am from the auto insurance agency or the car dealership. I feel my jaw clamp down. What do I say to a fool, I think. "Yes, my brother killed himself," I say. The attendant stops and points: "It's the white Dodge right over there." He turns away walking fast back to the office. The high sun squints off the metal side mirrors of the car parked clean and unmarred among others, like it is a day for a picnic and volleyball, and joy.

The things ... oh, not things. Artifacts. They are artifacts carefully spaced out on the front passenger seat, mementos and objects he left behind for the living. They are darts aimed at the eyes of our father, aimed at our hearts to make us bleed for our failures. There is the photograph of him and his four children, seated together and smiling one Christmas that we all spent at our sister's home on Long Island. Three girls and one boy, the youngest. His mother had become pregnant again less than a year after giving birth to the youngest girl. "I'm not ready," she protested. "But it might be a boy this time," we had urged. And so it was a boy who would grow up bitter without a father, blaming us, blaming me. We could not save my brother. But, during that holiday the boy was 8-years old and Jeff played with his son out in a smattering of new snow in the backyard of my sister's home and they built a 3-foot snowman.

On the seat, there is the military issue life insurance policy for his new wife and her phone number so she would be notified, and a partially empty Marlboro cigarette pack, and a novel from the library that I'm sure he hoped would offer respite from the torment. A single dark, round splotch of dried blood is on the fabric on the right shoulder of the driver's side. The police tell me he did it with a pearl-handled 32-caliber pistol notorious for spewing bullets that ricochet inside the skull and never exit. It was as if he didn't want to blow out the driver's side window, or damage the car. He would be a vegetable if he lived, they say. Later, his wife tells me the gun is hers and that through the night he made 200 calls to her from his cell phone, each no more than two seconds apart. The last one was as the sun rose in the humid mist of Indiana.

I gather the items from the car and return the keys to a young woman at the front counter. "I have everything," I say, without weeping. The other attendant is nowhere in sight.

Memory is unreliable because it is based on perception and not everything can be perceived all at once. There can be too much stimuli to recall everything accurately. I don't recall the name of the library book. I don't even know if I returned it or left it in the car. I know his wife and I found his Bible at the rooming house where he was staying. On a blank front page, he had used ink to write: "Help me, holy spirit." There are articles that are missed and incidents that are misunderstood. Was there really gravel in the parking lot? Were the items on the car seat laid out as if they were artifacts from an archaeological dig? Or had Jeff left the pieces there as if to say: "Here, you motherfuckers. See what you did. Here."

And that day, I didn't realize that his insurance policy would pay out the $250,000 benefit only to his new wife of four years and that his four underage children would receive nothing of the amount. And another thing I didn't realize then was that I shouldn't have left his athletic shoes in the trunk. I should have retrieved them also, even though they were muddy and beaten in. I didn't have the right to leave them. They belonged to his children. He was newly enlisted in the Army Reserve, with his new uniform in the shop having the strips and emblems sewn on it. At least, I did salvage his military boots and his dog tags. His life had been in motion. He had a good job as a draftsman in architecture which his colleagues told me he was really good at, a natural artist. But I didn't know that then and I didn't realize then he was paranoid schizophrenic, though for over ten years, he had been telling everyone that someone was following him. He couldn't understand why, and thought that perhaps he had inadvertently picked up some classified information when he was a Marine, though he was only a lance corporal and drove trucks. But maybe they thought he knew something. Or maybe it was his ex-wife. Maybe she was trying to find money to feed the four children she had birthed when they were married, all four children that he fathered. He would stare off as if he saw or heard something. In photographs of him, you can see him craning his head, cocking his ear as if someone called to him, or perhaps, as if a deep thought had just occurred to him, even though he held his infant son in his arms or sat among us laughing just moments before. Sometimes he would ask the person sitting next to him if they could hear the voices, too, saying: "Hear it? They're saying I'm a no good bastard, son of a bitching faggot," he'd say. And whoever sat next to him would tilt their head and strain their neck trying to hear. Eyebrows raised and ears poised. "No, I don't hear anything, J.D. [Jeff's preferred nickname]." Insistent, they say: "There's no one there, no one is there, J. D."

I do not know how this happens medically. I have some understanding of this abyss. If it was Post Traumatic Syndrome, it was not from war. He had never seen combat; he had been stationed in Okinawa as a Marine. There is no war there. His was a different trauma. He probably suffered multiple concussions after playing football from the time he reached puberty and throughout high school. He wanted to make our father proud.

Today, I am past menopause. My parents have passed on. Jeffrey's four young adult children have shut me out of their lives. I know nothing of the life he had made with his second wife. I could be counted on to pick up the pieces, like medicine after the fact when preventative care has been neglected. I saw what was done to Jeff. I did some of it myself. This memory is typical for families that have experienced sudden tragedy. It's unplanned and the incredible sadness is beyond measure. I think of the parents of the little children that are killed in schools in our country. You dress them up in their freshly laundered OshKosh B'gosh school clothes or their uniforms and you send them off to a fun day of crayons and coloring, recess, and learning the alphabet and how to add and subtract and do multiplication, but they never come home. How can you possibly bear up to that?

Families suffer in silence. It seems that advocating for better treatment for mental health should get more funding. Sometimes I think football and basic training and soldiering may have something in common in what can happen to the brain of a young man or woman. I've read that when it comes to soldiers, there is an enormous suicide rate outside the usual rate. And now we know that Chronic Traumatic Encephalopathy (CTE) causes brain damage and several athletes have committed suicide after experiencing CTE. If I could change anything, it would be to never have to go to the police pound to retrieve the artifacts of my younger brother's forty year life. I would make it so that the police came by the cemetery before he could raise the gun to his temple. And they would tell him to move along and he would awaken from the dark. I would change it so that his wife answered her phone, even though it would only be temporary without help. But he had visited our father days earlier and he had said he was going for help. There is still more to say, but it has been 20 years now. So, you bear up. You finish the course.

—m—

Mr. West (by author Sarah Blake)

A declared lover of hip-hop, Sarah Blake chose to explore the public life of Kanye West for her debut collection, *Mr. West,* a bold, original, and innovative exercise in contemporary poetry. In this slim volume of six chapters and forty-six poems, Blake surveys Kanye West's public life from inside out in this lyric biography. Blake has been an editor at Saturnalia Books and has been published in the *Threepenny Review* and the *Boston Review.* She also received funding for the work from a NEA Literature Fellowship.

When asked why she chose West as a subject, Blake said she connected with the artist, despite their difference in gender and race, as she privately grieved over the loss of her beloved grandfather through her art. The timing coincided with West's public grief over the death of his mother expressed in his album *808s & Heartbreak.* The collection's unorthodox, bold originality focuses on topics about West often unrelated to music, but specifically related to what Zapruder called an identifiable situation. Blake's situation was that of a new, mother-to-be immersed in pop culture research, and who once taught sixth graders about the digestive system. She draws on this background in the lineated free verse poem Kanye's Digestive System. Writing "I love the digestive system," she lists the parts of our stomachs noting how long the small intestine is after death: "The length of the letters individually undone in this very book!/The length of my cooing for Kanye!" (17). Subsequent chapters also describe functions of the human body.

Rather than death, in Kanye's Skeletal System, Blake

lists parts of the human skeleton and tells the reader that "First, a baby will have a skeleton completely/of cartilage./In the fourth month of pregnancy, it begins to turn to bone./And then I'll hold onto those bones forever./ Kanye, I could tell you so many more things about the bones (26)." Finally, in Kanye's Circulatory System which Blake said was the first poem she wrote about West, she connects again for the anniversary of the death of her grandfather to write about the death of Kanye's mother, Donda West, referring to when she tutored a sixth-grader on the heart and addressing Kanye with: "I'd love if you'd recorded a song. I almost forget again that your heart/ looks like mine/ . . . . You miss her and I miss him but/ surely I cannot say if, when you think of death, you, Kanye, think of the/heart (42)."

Blake wrote two letters in her collection. Dear Kanye, in a prose poem and Dear Donda in a four-part free verse poem, in which she wonders what Dr. West would think about her and other white women. In the fantastical letter to Kanye, she imagines tree branches as fingers running along the top of Kanye's head in the manner of one who loves you. "Are they not the fingers that begin to resemble your mothers? only to end with I realize some days I shouldn't write about you (77)." Indeed, in a passage of this sort even Blake seems to understand she may have crossed a line.

Crossing this line could be where the book may falter for readers as it did for me. It seemed to take liberties that felt intrusive. It could be perceived as the kind of co-opting that Morgan Parker objects to when it comes to Black celebrities, and Black life, in general. Parker's work is situated in pop culture also and she wrote of such audacity in the chapter "Two White Girls in the African Braid Shop on Marcy and Fulton" in her latest work, *Magical Negro*: "Can I ask is that a weave. . . .Where's your real hair." Or as Rankine laments, "you there, hey you."

Still, Blake answers in Dear Donda: "When I wanted to put my fingers in your hair, I wasn't saying, *can I touch it?/I was saying caress* (52)." Later in the collection, she acknowledge her white privilege in the poem "Gaze: A white pregnant woman has privilege but also shortness of breath (89)."

Finally, in the poem Like the Poems Do (10), Blake wrote of retiring for the night to the bedroom with her husband: "Noah lets me/bring Kanye in,/knows our life has room for all of it." The book is dedicated to Kanye and to Noah.

Blake, Sarah. *Mr. West.* Wesleyan University Press, 2015.
     https://sarahblakeauthor.com/mr-west/
     https://mrwest.sarahblakepoetry.com/
Jerkins, Morgan. Midnight at the Greatest Party of All Time. *Poetry.*
     https://www.poetryfoundation.org/articles/149145/ midnight-at-the-greatest-party-of-all-time.
Parker, Morgan. Two White Girls in the African Braid Shop on Marcy and Fulton. *Magical Negro.* New York: Tin house Books, 2019, p. 31. Kindle Edition.
Rankine, Claudia. Some years there exists a wanting to escape. Graywolf Press, 2014, pp 139-146.
Zapruder, Matthew. Show Your Work! *Poetry.*
     https://www.poetryfoundation.org/articles/69287/ show-your-work

Charisma

Charisma Defined

Since the early 20th century, the idea of charisma has been especially associated with German sociologist, Max Weber. Lepsius (2006) notes that Weber considered charisma a revolutionary force and adds that the associated charismatic relationship between gifted leaders and their followers fundamentally restructures a given social situation. Weber proposed that charisma, though widely discussed in sociology, psychology, political science, communication, and other disciplines, is considered an elusive, concept and often described as a special quality some people possess that allows them to relate to and affect others at a deep emotional level (Riggio, 1998). Both adherents *and* opponents react emotionally to charismatic leaders. The enthusiasm of one group's responses is matched by the mistrust of the other group (House, 1977).

In addition, for charisma to function there has to be an emotional arousal among followers (Willner, 1984). This strong and complete emotional commitment to the leader and his or her vision is expressed by followers in their ideas and their actions. For example, devotees of King, Roosevelt, and Gandhi all expressed adoration, reverence, and vows of lifelong allegiance, often making frenzied attempts to see, touch, reach the 'person' of the leader, and gesturing as if to worship (Willner, 1984). They may consider objects the leader has touched as sacred. The maintenance of emotional arousal is pertinent to the long-term success of the charismatic leader.

Charismatic Authority

Charismatic leaders are said to arise during environmental movements for change. Weber's main focus was on the emergence of such leaders during certain crises. He found that charisma and personality blend most readily in times of psyche, physical, economic, ethical, religious, political distress (Eisenstadt, 1968). Erik H. Erikson suggests that large numbers of people become charisma hungry under certain conditions in which religion wanes, and that charismatic leaders minister well during three kinds of distress: the condition of fear; the condition of anxiety (with that being the unease of people no longer knowing who they are and creating an identity vacuum and anxiety), with the third condition being existential dread (Eatwell, 2006). In this type of distress, people experience circumstances in which the rituals of their human existence become dysfunctional. *Deep social change presents a crisis.* Under such situations, a charismatic leader may emerge to provide a coalescing sense of solidarity among populations. By offering perceived salvation from fear, anxiety and existential dread, the charismatic leader brings new forms of identity, often reinforced by rituals that give feelings of well-being and safety (Eatwell, 2006).

The emergent charismatic leader is considered more effective than leaders in non-crisis situations. Thus, charismatic movements are mostly likely to develop and multiply when there is widespread distress in society. The charismatic leader promises the hope of salvation and the nature of the dynamic between the leader and the followers is specifically messianic (Pillai, 1996). He or she is the savior who has risen to lead people from the present distress.

The Charismatic Bond

In his examination of charismatic authority, Weber conceded that charismatic individuals possessed extraordinary qualities that captivated others, but went further to determine that the emergence and operation of charisma was, in fact, found within the bond between the leader and his or her followers (Riggio, 1998). Modern theories of charismatic leadership hold fast to Weber's theory that the connection between the leader and follower is fundamental to understanding charisma. Charismatic leadership appears, and is authenticated and established within the leader's interactions with followers or devotees.

Charisma is a quality that can so enamor others that they will often follow a charismatic leader without question. The followers magnify the leader's power. They have put their trust in the leader, who will somehow take care of things, (Berkley and Rouse, 2009). There is a sense of invulnerability and the leader is considered godlike; she or he is a savior, linked to Jesus or other sacred figures (Willner, 1984).

Lepsius (2006) describes Weber's model of charismatic authority as a combination of personal devotion and duty to a leader who has arisen to claim ultimate authority, indeed has demanded it, and as their duty the followers are compelled to submit completely to the leader in obedience—so that it is not only charisma that is an extraordinary quality: charismatic relationships are also extraordinary. Charismatic leadership is legitimate domination, granted by the followers who believe in the virtues of the leader and value his or her leadership (Lepsius, 2006). The individual that embodies charismatic authority is able to stir the idea and the acceptance of having legitimate dominion within his or her own system or sphere of influence.

> The charismatic hero does not deduce his authority from codes and statutes, as is the case with the jurisdiction of office; nor does he deduce his authority from traditional custom or ritual of faith (Eisenstadt, 1968).

Nor will the leader's conduct conform to organizational controls. Lepsius (2006) asserts that charismatic relationships do not follow any institutional criteria for rationality. A leader aspiring for this ultimate authority carves out a unique role or position that only he or she can fill. The social position will be different for followers as well (Lepsius, 2006). Weber observed that charisma is best understood as a social relationship (Lepsius, 2006). Lepsius (2006) maintains that the social group formed around charismatic leadership is an emotional community bound by personal devotion to the leader.

Weber and other theorists consider the existence of charismatic authority unstable because to maintain charismatic authority, the leader must continue to prove his or her strength to the faithful followers by performing what are perceived as heroic deeds or miracles (Eisenstadt, 1968). Charismatic leaders have authority only because pure charisma is legitimized from personal strength and from the gift within – which must constantly be proven (Eisenstadt, 1968).

> Messianic hopes do not completely eliminate the perception of reality in the interests of followers. If charisma disappears, the charismatic relationship vanishes completely. This is the greatest obligation that the charismatic leader has: he must prove himself (Lepsius, 2006).

The followers must benefit by adhering to the tenets of the mission, or they will withdraw and stop following. In that case, the leader may feel as though the God who gifted him or her has withdrawn favor. The leader is at risk of losing the charisma if deserted by his following. The mission is aborted and the followers are set adrift, as if without a rudder.

Charisma Lost

Weber asserted that the charismatic leader who comes under fire must make sure his or her followers do not become distressed (Eisenstadt, 1968). If they do, then the duty of the leader is to take the charge for any real or perceived failings. The penalty for the breach may include exile. Sometimes, it may even be death. With his influence diluted and his reputation in tatters, the pure charismatic will 'deport himself.' If this banishment does not restore the former glory, the charismatic hero 'faces dispossession and death, each often enough is consummated as a propitiatory sacrifice' (Eisenstadt, 1968). Nevertheless, Lepsius (2006) asserts that, charisma can be sustained even in case of failure if the causes of these failures can be attributed to others. This is especially true when the followers through enthusiasm or necessity and hope do not want to let go (Lepsius, 2006). "Failed prophecies can still be believed; former proofs can be reexamined. And perhaps the former glories can return."

Bibliography for Charisma

Berkley, G. and Rouse, J. (2009). Communication and Leadership. *The Craft of Public Administration.* Tenth Edition. New York: McGraw-Hill, pp. 218-224.

Eatwell, R. (2006). The Concept and Theory of Charismatic Leadership./Totalitarian Movements & Political Religions, 7(2), 141-156.

Eisenstadt, S. N. (1968). Max Weber: On charisma and institution building. Chicago: University of Chicago Press

House, R.J., and J.M. Howell (1992) "Personality and Charismatic Leadership," *The Leadership Quarterly* 3, 81-108.

House, R.J., and B. Shamir (1993) "Toward the Integration of Charismatic, Transformational and Visionary Theories," in M.M. Chemers and R. Ayman (eds.), *Leadership Theory and Research: Perspectives and Directions*, New York: Academic Press.

House, R. J., & Shamir, B. 1993. Toward the integration of charismatic, visionary and transformational leadership theories. In M. M. Chemers & R. Ayman (Eds.), Leadership theory and research: Perspectives and directions: 81-107. San Diego: Academic Press.

House, R.J., W.D. Spangler, and J. Woycke (1991) A Personality and Charisma in the U.S. Presidency: A Psychological Theory of Leadership Effectiveness," *Administrative Science Quarterly* 36, 364-396.

Lepsius, M. (2006). The Model of Charismatic Leadership and its Applicability to the Rule of Adolf Hitler. Totalitarian Movements & Political Religions, 7(2), 175-190.

Pillai, R. and J.R. Meindl (1991) "The Effect of a Crisis on the Emergence of Charismatic Leadership: A Laboratory Study," *Academy of Management Best Paper Proceedings*, 235-239.

Riggio, R. E. (1998). Charisma. In H. S. Friedman (Ed.), Encyclopedia of mental health (pp. 387-396). San Diego, CA: Academic Press.

Weber, M., (1968). In S. N. Eisenstadt, (Ed.), Max Weber on charisma and institution building: Selected papers. University of Chicago Press.

Willner, A.R. (1984) *The Spellbinders: Charismatic Political Leadership*, New Haven, CT: Yale University Press.

Bring the Colored People

"My name is Amelia Crockett. I'm a 92-year-old colored woman. I was born in Hinton, West Virginia, but because my daddy, Mr. William Crockett, is a Pullman Porter we moved to Peru, Indiana, when I was 12. The railroad was in Peru and so was the circus. Peru, Indiana is the circus capital of the world and everybody knows it.

"But one thing I'm really proud of is that I been faithfully attending Allen Chapel A.M.E. church for 50 years, longer than anyone else that goes there. And I love my church. I'm so glad that in the summer of 1794, long before I was born, Richard Allen, the first black Methodist minister, founded Bethel AME (African Methodist Episcopal) church. He wouldn't have done it necessarily, but after the controversy his spirit in him was highly disturbed. See, the yellow fever had come to the city just in the last year, in '93 and everybody was dying and people were getting out of the city and the mayor come and ask minister Allen and his associate to bring the colored people to come and nurse the sick and bury the dead. As for me, I don't know why the mayor thought it would make sense to do that when there was so many more white people. Story goes that the city officials thought the coloreds were immune to the disease. But I don't believe the story.

"So, anyway, minister Allen had been preaching to the coloreds for five a.m. services in the separate area of the commons near St. George's Methodist Episcopal Church in

Philadelphia Pennsylvania. Many people came back to hear minister Allen preach.

One day, I remember we were sitting in chairs along the wall because we can sit in the pews. There were a lot of people and it was getting full and so they started to sit in some of the new pews because they didn't know the pews were reserved for the whites. Then, when we was kneeling in prayer, a trustee came over and grabbed minister Allen's associate, Absalom Jones, and told him to get up. "You can't kneel here," he said. We all looked up from our prayer."

"Please, wait till the prayer is over," Mr. Jones told him. "No, you have to get up or I will call for help and force you out," the trustee said. Well, we couldn't believe we were being treated this way because we too are brethren in the Christian faith. So, we hurried to finish our prayers and then we got up and left and we never came back.

So, that was when minister Allen decided we would have our own church and it would be called African Methodist Episcopal Church. And, then there are more controversies, but eventually minister Allen was consecrated as the first black bishop in the United States of America, and today the AME church is in North America, the Caribbean, sub-Saharan Africa and parts of South America, and has over 2 million members.

African Methodist Episcopal Church
https://en.wikipedia.org/wiki/African_Methodist_
Episcopal_Church#Overview
Bishop Richard Allen: Apostle of Freedom
https://www.ame-church.com/founders-day-2018/
https://www.ame-church.com/our-church/our-
history/
History of Peru, Indiana
https://indianahistory.org/wp-content/uploads/peru-
indiana-copy-photographs.pdf

Bare and Silent

I have been silenced. Silenced in the way I silenced my elders when I was still a fool. What could they offer with their rumpled shuffling, their padded flesh, their pastel-colored comfort clothing. I was busy. I had goals, places to go in pursuit of the future, foregoing the joy of the process and the present. I would be satisfied once I obtained the riches beyond the present. It was gonna be great.

Now, I am silent when among fools. What can they offer me with their platitudes and advices I learned long ago, some of which I no longer care to observe. But how can they know? They are busy. They have places to go. I have been silenced. Only love, and patience, and affection speak now. They are adorable, and sometimes insufferable.

I am older. I have regrets that I try to forgive myself for, though I am reminded daily what has brought me to these spare, lean times. I try daily to replace regret with thankfulness that I am well enough, nourished enough, clothed enough, warm enough. able enough. I have no need, only desire.

Still I am patronized and ignored. But no one can tell exactly what it is when I show vigor and wear black. It appears all is well, and though in reality that is true, there remains a desire for that touch I once so enjoyed. Do not look at me and turn away. It used to break my heart when that happened. I remember when you whistled your appreciation and I did not mind. Now, I won't cause you to wonder so that you peer toward me for a glimpse until I turn and you turn away. Now,

I go out bare so you will not look at me. Eyelashes do not flutter, cheeks are not flushed, lips do not beckon. Now, I am invisible. And, if I speak you might patronize. So, I may not speak so much, but soft, flat, or I am silent.

We Won't Go

It's 2:00 p. m. on a Tuesday afternoon and political science professor Dr. Jack Smith stands in front of the classroom door, as if he's not sure he is in the right place on the first floor of the stone-faced Ballinger building, named after a prominent alum who gave generously, but would die before the semester was over. His right-hand trembles as he begins to introduce himself to the class, just as he has done with every new group of students, each new semester for his almost 40 years at Medina State University. Mostly from small towns in southern Ohio, the recent batch of undergraduate students sit in groups of three or four among the metal desks arranged in a grid. His graduate teaching assistant sits on the other side of the room under a bank of windows overlooking the campus grounds.

"Hello, class. My name is Dr. Jack Smith as you can see on your syllabus I look forward to a productive learning experience with you this semester. Over to my left is my graduate assistant, Molly Vincent, whom I understand has already introduced herself to you." Then, Smith holds up a book.

"This is the textbook titled *Public Administration for the 20th Century* that I wrote and that we'll be using. Please get yours from the bookstore, or somewhere else. It's on Amazon. Then read the Introduction and Chapter One. And by the way, it's the student's responsibility to learn from what takes place in any classroom, not that of the professor. That's all for today. I'll see you Thursday. Oh, and don't forget to sign the attendance sheet going around. Molly will collect it."

As Professor Smith leaves the room, Molly says, "Hey everybody, I keep office hours from 2-4 p.m. every day if you want to stop by with any questions or concerns. It's on the lower level in Room B10." Molly picks up the attendance sheet. She waits for the room to empty before leaving.

Chairperson Ben Tulley scans the performance evaluations for the professors in his department and frowns. Provost Blake Walker appears at his open door, walks in and sits down in front of his desk.

"Hey, Ben, I wanted to ask you to keep in mind that I'm pushing for a low performance policy that would allow the university to more easily fire even tenured professors with unsatisfactory performance," he said.

Ben takes off his reading classes. "Well, sure. I do want to support you but if that kind of policy is adopted I can see where we'll be losing one or two colleagues from this department. Jack would be at the top of the list. Look at these student comments on his evaluation."

Ben hands Blake the report:

"The instructor was extremely forgetful and did not stimulate conversation well or listen to students opinions very well."

"Professor Smith is a creature of another time period. He is an old school professor who has refused to change his teaching methods to actually help students learn about public administration. I hope this will be Professor Smith's last semester here at Medina State."

"Professor Smith was very hard to understand because of his stuttering and mumbling. I feel as though this professor should have retired long ago."

Professor Smith wrote the textbook we have to use, it cost $90 and it's out-of-date."

"Doctor Smith is very intelligent but is also very old and loses his train of thought often. Many times he can't remember his point and moves on, which confuses the class. But he has lots of wisdom and good stories. His travel experiences are very interesting."

This is a difficult review because Doctor Smith seems like a nice man with infinite amounts of knowledge to share with his students, but it just never seemed to make its way into the classroom."

Blake shook his head as he handed the paper back. "My God, Ben, this is truly concerning. What is going on with Jack anyway?

"Not sure. He told me he's seeing a neurologist when I asked him how he was feeling. I haven't yet talked to him about his evaluation though.

"I know we opened a search three months ago to add another public administration professor. How is the search going? Have you been interviewing?"

"Yes, and so far we've rejected three candidates, and made one offer that was turned down. So, it's slow going,"

The provost stands up to leave. "All right, just keep me informed. We'll meet next week to hash it out more."

The next day, a headline in the *Star Press* read: "State University to weed out lazy professors." "This is for chronic low performers," Blake told the newspaper. Most are older, and have been at Medina State for decades, the report said.

Professor Smith's elbows are on his desk and his head in his hands as sits in his office. His vintage 1980s Harvest yellow desk chair creaks with each shift of his weight. He's logged into his e-mail where he has just received his copy of the performance report Ben Tulley has submitted to the dean's office. When Molly arrives, he hands her the printout. Molly, a woman in her early 40s, is working on a master's degree in public administration. He considers her more of a confidante than a grad student needing mentoring. Smith is 71.

"I can't believe Ben wrote such a negative final report. We've been working in the same department ever since he came on board some 20 years ago," Smith says.

After spending decades as a university professor, Smith is struggling with the realization that his career is ending. Colleagues are urging him to retire, but his wife, Betty, wants him to keep working to support her love of travel.

Frustrated, he says, "on top of that, I've been assigned two new courses for next semester. That load is too heavy, and Ben knows it." He unfolds his lanky frame from the chair in the cramped office. He has taught two course sections, five days a week, for the past ten years using the textbook he wrote. That was the last time he constructed a new syllabus and lesson plans. He has not yet taught an online course.

"This is how they try to shove you out. Molly. But I'm not ready to go."

Molly nods her head. "Do you want me to pull subject journal articles for you to review in preparation for teaching the courses?" Just recently she was talking with Gloria, another nontraditional student, about the 1996 Supreme Court ruling that said forced retirement is age discrimination. Now older faculty members were choosing to stay on the job as long as possible, some of them earning six figures or more, even at public institutions. The women wondered what that would mean for them.

"Yeah, that will help. Also, pull some public administration studies in immersive learning." Smith pauses. "It's my identity, Molly. What will I do? I won't have anything to do. . . I might die," he says.

Smith leans forward with his head bent low as he walks down the hall. He wants to avoid eye contact with others. His steps are quick, each one a bird-like hop. He says he walks with a bounce in his step after having his knees replaced. Recently, he has been diagnosed with Parkinson's disease. Today, he is headed for assistant professor Steve Pollock's office when he bumps into him.

"Oh hey, Steve, I was just on my way to your office." Smith casually leans against the wall, his belly protruding over his belt. "They're trying to shove me out, Steve." Smith's voice rises sounding wounded.

"Oh yeah?"

"Yeah, they gave me all these courses. What is 466? I never heard of it," Smith says.

"Haven't heard of it either," Steve replies. "Must be new; probably has a technology component, is my guess."

"Well, I gotta find out who's behind this sabotage." Smith turns to head back down the hall, arms swinging to the rhythm of his steps.

Early on a Saturday morning, Smith sent Chris Johnson in Student Life an email message: "Mr. Johnson," he said, "I would like to commence discussions for an immersive learning project. We need to make connections between the city and the University student population. I will call you Monday."

Monday afternoon, after having spoken to Johnson, Smith sent another message: "Feel free to invite others to our 2 p.m. session Tuesday. The policymaking must be mutual between the City Council and the mayor and student groups." Smith also sent a copy of the message to Dr. Tim James in the History department. "Tim, can you meet with Chris Johnson and I tomorrow at 2:00 p.m.? We need to discuss ideas for immersive learning that I first brought up with city officials several years ago."

Smith contacted the mayor's office and the City Council president, inviting them to meet him and Chris, a slender young black man, and Tim, the curly haired history professor, at the Office of Student Affairs in the student center Chris and Tim were first to show up for the meeting. After the men exchanged pleasantries, Chris asked Tim, "do you know what the meeting is about?" His look was quizzical behind his wire-rimmed glasses.

"No, I was hoping you knew," Tim said, also bewildered about why he was there.

Just then, Smith arrived and after a collegial greeting, the two men said, "what are we meeting about, Jack?" Before Smith could answer the two officials arrived from city government.

"What's this all about?" the city council member asked.

"Well, I don't have a solid idea, but I think university students should work with the city," Smith blurted out.

The four people fell silent. They knew Smith well and had come to meet with him out of respect. But it was obvious he had shown up with no concrete ideas. The group batted about some ideas and Chris politely assured Jack that the city and university already worked together.

Dr. Sheila Dotson of the mayor's office suggested: "Your students can come and have lunch with the mayor."

So, the group made promises to follow up. and the short, awkward meeting ended.

News of the incident surfaced several days later, when Tim told the chair of his department that through a series of emails and voicemail messages, Smith had invited him to the meeting. "I thought it was because Jack knew I figured prominently in the university's immersive learning initiative, and he wanted to meet about an idea he had for his courses. But he had no real agenda for the meeting. I'm concerned the University looks unprepared and clueless when we have this type of contact with community leaders," Tim explained.

Smith's reprimand came swiftly in a letter on the university's official letterhead. "I was called into his office. I was given the reprimand. It was already a done deal," Smith tells Molly. "He put it in my permanent file without talking to me first or giving me a chance to explain what happened. "Smith waves a hand toward a table where the document is lying. It reads:

"This behavior is inexcusable on a number of grounds... you have embarrassed our department...this episode raises questions about your judgment, especially in your field. You must immediately cease any unauthorized outreach to the community in your role as a member of this department. This letter will be placed in your permanent file. You have the option to reply in writing and include your reply in your file as well." In response, Smith writes a rebuttal letter to the chair and releases it into the "public domain" for dissemination.

The next day, Smith encounters Steve in the hallway. "Good to see you, Jack. Hey, the administration office released the fall schedule. Come to find out all of us have got extra courses for next semester. The hiring committee couldn't fill the department's two open professorships. Can't find anybody who wants to be in southern Ohio, and when we do, we can't pay them enough," Steve blurts out with a hearty laugh. "'Ironic, huh," he says.

Smith is stunned but collects himself. "No kidding. Fair enough, Steve. Good to know." Smith manages to smile before walking off. He returns to his office and closes the door that he normally leaves open for his graduate assistants and for students who want to come by. He sits down at his desk and begins to type a letter to Ben but then stops and shuts down his laptop. He locks up his office and leaves the building.

One week after the semester ended, Smith and his wife, Betty, left for Australia. When he returns in the fall, he is scheduled to teach two new classes along with his regular class. Before leaving the country, he paid the $2000 premium to keep his long-term care insurance in force in case he will need assistance as the Parkinson's disease progresses and the dementia worsens.

Before he left he told Molly, "I'm going to spend time determining the extent of my Parkinson's disease and the dementia and how it affects my behavior. I've got tests scheduled."

Two years later, upon his retirement, Dr. Jack Smith wrote:
"My parting consciousness and awareness and thoughts on students are directed specifically to students but are applicable to anyone at any stage of life. So here goes. Follow directions, read widely, follow road signs in life, do basics well, directly engage institutions, ideas and people. Act on the premises of free speech. Create personal passions and chase after them. Observe and question culture. Culture liberates and binds. Tell the truth. Don't cheat. It's better to fail than cheat. Life is full of failures. The important part is getting up to toil., to create, to rise again."

THE END

Acknowledgements

I want to acknowledge and thank the women in my life who stood by me, encouraged me, believed in me, and who even gave me bodily shelter sometimes during my wandering travels. You know who you are. Thank you Cindy B., Stephanie B., Ava B., Betty C., Martha C., Melanie F., Georgia H., Vanessa H., Cheryl S., Vicky S., Denise T., Gia W., Sandy W., Juliet W., Susan W., Lori W., Holly W., Barbara W., and Eloise W. I love you all.

Printed in the United States
by Baker & Taylor Publisher Services